Thank You for the Strawberries

To the people in my life I am most grateful for –
who know why this book could not be about blueberries.

ISBN 978-1986096034

Library of Congress Control Number 2018902754

"Thank you for the strawberries Mom," said Zoe.

Zoe's favorite fruit is strawberries.

She likes to eat them

with her cereal in the morning

and in her yogurt.

Strawberry ice cream
is her favorite flavor.

Zoe likes strawberry jam

and strawberry shortcake.

She likes their deep red color,

their sweet smell,

and delicious flavor.

She also likes the way the strawberry seeds tickle her tongue.

"Zoe it's my pleasure
to wash and serve you strawberries,"
said her mother.

"Let's thank Daddy

who bought them from the store,

and the storekeeper
who stocked the shelves
with strawberries,

and the truck driver

who transported them

from the farm to the supermarket,

and the workers

who picked the strawberries,

packaged them,

and loaded them onto the truck.

Let's also appreciate the farmers
who planted the strawberry seeds in the ground
and watered them,

and the sun, earth, wind and rain,

which helped the strawberries grow,

and let's give thanks

for the miracle of strawberries

which we enjoy."

Zoe whispered thank you

to all the people

who took part in bringing her

the sweet, delicious strawberries.

Riki Lax is a speech therapist who lives in California, New York, and Miami. She loves to travel, teach, and eat strawberries.

Riki enjoys reading books to children and using books to teach communication skills and life lessons.

Get her free resources on how to use this book
to develop your children's and students' 21st Century Skills
- the skills they need to thrive in today's world -
at
thankyouforthestrawberries.com

Made in United States
North Haven, CT
27 November 2021